Advance

"*God's Mountain*, a Japanese folk tale, illustrates the persona of love and the importance of family. Along with the suspenseful adventures of the hero Kenji and his mother Miyuki, we get to witness the time of the samurai. This is an enjoyable story about a time that is unfamiliar to most of us. I recommend it."

-Kay Brownlow

"A tender novel of family love, sacrifice and blessing based on Japanese custom of the samurai time."

-Gaile Turnbull

"*God's Mountain* is a wonderful collection of stories of old people who go to the God's Mountain to die! Some great lessons are learned by people willing to follow their heart."

-Barbara & Bob French

"This historical fiction is quite enjoyable for all ages. Following a woman from her parents' death to her own death and spiritual destiny is a story well told."

-William Charles Hall

Acknowledgments

I want to give a special word of thanks to many of my friends.

Thank you to Kathryn Brownlow, my counselor, a beautiful, humble, and intelligent writer.

Thank you to Dr. Bill Ruehlmann, who helped me add the final touch to this story.

Thank you to Mr. and Mrs. Ed Bacon, Gil Erb, who loved this and gave good advice.

Members of the Virginia Beach Writers, Hampton Roads Writers, Great Neck Book Club, and First Colonial Inn Writers always gave good advice.

Thank you to my dear friends, Gaile Turnbull, Mr. and Mrs. David and Barbara French, Mr. William Charles Hall, Louise Wilson, and Joan Uhlar who read my manuscripts and gave me excellent opinions.

Thank you to Larry Elliot, Dr. David G. Clark, Rev. Kiyoomi Tsujimoto, Rev. Shinichi and Shizu Fukiage, Lauran Strait, Linda Cobb, Cynthia Halliday, Anne Westrick, Dr. Dennis Bond, and LCDR Ed DeLong.

Thank you to John Koehler, who encouraged me to write *God's Mountain*.

Thank you to J. Thomas Hetrick, my wonderful publisher.

May God bless all.

God's Mountain

Midori Bamba

Pocol Press
Clifton, VA

"The glory of young men is their strength; of old men, their experience."
Proverbs 20:29

May God Bless you,
Midori Bamba

POCOL PRESS

Published in the United States of America
by Pocol Press
6023 Pocol Drive
Clifton, VA 20124
www.pocolpress.com

**Publisher's
Cataloguing-in-Publication data**

Bamba, Midori, 1948-
  God's mountain / Midori Bamba.
  p. cm.
  ISBN 978-1-929763-51-1
1. Samurai--Fiction. 2. Japan—History—Tokugawa period,
1600-1868--Fiction. 3. Historical fiction. I. Title

PS35522.A47312 G36 2013
813.54--dc23   201295594

Library of Congress Control Number: 2012955594

Art by Alexander.

Prologue

In the late afternoon, a son and a father walked on the mountain path. Neither of them spoke. The son, who looked to be in his mid-forties of medium size and well-muscled, had eyes as dark as a bottomless swamp. He tried not to cry, but he sobbed bitterly.

The sky was as blue as the sapphire; flowers bloomed and birds sang cheerfully. Tree leaves had just begun to turn golden yellow, but the young man didn't notice this autumn mountain beauty. His heart was heavy as sand, and his face was pale as paper.

Once in a while, he looked at his father, who dropped white petals from his sack and threw them on the path.

Father must want to return home so he drops these flowers as a mark, the son thought, and he felt sorry for him.

My father is seventy, but he is still so healthy and strong. He is a wonderful father! The son sighed.

He taught me to be a man.

He protected me from wild animals when they attacked me.

He saved me from drowning when I was a child.

He taught me how to plant, how to cut the wood, how to swim...

1

He taught me all his wisdom and experience and how to be a mature man.

His mind is still as sharp as a sword.

Why do I have to send him to God's Mountain?

His every step was heavy, as if he wore lead shoes. His sight was blurred.

How long had they walked? At last they reached God's Mountain.

Oh! the son gasped. He heard the black birds' weird song. The slope became steep. They began to climb.

Slowly, the father stopped walking and pointed to a flat stone. The son nodded and put a straw mat on the stone. Father waved his hand, his face pale as if he were already dead. But his son didn't want to leave and stood still. They looked at each other for a long time. Black birds flew around as if they were waiting for something. Finally, the sun set, and it got dark and chilly. A cold wind started to blow. *My father will be cold tonight*, the son thought. When people went to God's Mountain, they were not allowed to bring a warm kimono. Father waved his hand again, so his son glanced at his father one last time and turned away from him. But it was so dark and he couldn't see the way back. He was panicked, until he saw white petals on the ground. *These petals are to guide me home safely.* The son felt his father's deep love.

A long time ago in Japan, there was God's Mountain. In that time, there was often not enough precious food for everyone; therefore, older people had to go to God's Mountain to die in order to let their children eat the scarce food available.

It was sad, but some older parents showed their love in the last minutes of their lives.

God's Mountain, they felt, led you to an extraordinarily fertile and more beautiful world.

1
A Quiet Snow Day

There were mountains and mountains. A village was located between those mountains. This village has no name; therefore, other village people, across one mountain, called this village "other village." Miyuki lived in an old house at the end of "other village."

Tiny ants were walking on the ground, each one carrying a heavy load. Miyuki watched them. Her cheeks were pink as peaches, her skin as white as snow. Her dark brown intelligent eyes sparkled beautifully above her little pug nose. Her blue cotton kimono was simple, but she was a healthy happy child. Wind blew her straight black hair.

"What are you watching?" asked Grandmother.

Miyuki looked at her, smiling. Grandmother smiled back. She came close to Miyuki and stood beside her. She gently stroked Miyuki's head.

"Do you see how these tiny ants work?" Miyuki asked, her eyes still fixed on these ants.

"Miyuki, these tiny ants teach us a great lesson. They are small, but they work together to save food for winter." Grandmother's voice was soft and warm like a spring sun.

"Grandmother, ants are smart, aren't they?"

Grandmother nodded and said, "Unless you are faithful in small matters, you won't be faithful in large ones."

Miyuki's mother died when she was an infant, so Grandmother raised her. Miyuki learned how to sew, cook and gained much wisdom from her grandmother. Grandmother didn't know how to write or read, but she was wise and an excellent teacher. She had learned from her experience and taught her all wisdom to Miyuki, and Miyuki was a good listener.

Miyuki returned her eyes to the ants that worked hard, carrying food.

"I taught you everything I knew. Do not forget my teaching and take care of your father." Grandmother's voice was soft and gentle like a bamboo flute.

"Oh, Grandmother, you are so beautiful in your white kimono. You look like a snow fairy," Miyuki said and touched her white kimono sleeve with her small hands.

"Yes, I am going to God's Mountain." Her dark eyes and Miyuki's innocent eyes met. Overwhelmed with sorrow, Grandmother remained standing still.

"Can I go with you?" asked Miyuki.

"Not now, my child," she said and crawled to Miyuki and hugged her to her chest one last time.

Miyuki never forgot the night she saw Grandmother in her white kimono. She was carried by her son, Miyuki's father, and left the house at midnight. Miyuki said goodbye to her grandmother silently. It was a cold night, but her feelings were numb. She looked at her grandmother for a long time -- her shadow became smaller and smaller, and then they disappeared in the dark night. How long did she stand in the darkness? Then she realized that she was surrounded by snow; it touched her hair, cheeks and kimono gently, as if the snowflakes comforted her. Snowflakes danced in the cold air and fell on tree branches, roofs and all over the ground, as if a snow fairy spread a white veil. Miyuki breathed deeply.

"Grandmother, you are like a snow fairy -- gentle, delicate and beautiful. I am glad it snowed on your last day," Miyuki murmured.

Miyuki's grandmother loved snow, so she named her Miyuki, which means beautiful deep snow. Miyuki imagined her grandmother lying in the snow, her face pale, her body like ice, snow continuing to fall on her until it buried her.

Miyuki went out into the dark and lay on the snow. "Good-bye, Grandmother. I am glad it snowed. Someday, we will see each other again. Please visit me after you become a snow fairy. Good-bye…"

Miyuki remembered Grandmother's words: "Snow absorbs sound, so a snow day is very quiet." Miyuki felt she was surrounded by a deadly silence.

Tears froze on her cheeks.

2
The Wedding Gifts

Morning dew sparkled all over the field like tears of crystal. Seeds that the wind brought grew, and many wildflowers bloomed everywhere. The sun was warm and fresh; the morning air rustled like whispers. It was a beautiful spring morning.

Miyuki was picking buttercups in the field. Her small hands moved busily as she made a crown. She arranged wild purple flowers in between the buttercups. Today was her big sister's wedding day. She thought she wanted to give her a wedding gift, so she got up at sunrise and came to the field. There was no wedding ceremony in this poor village. A bride just moved to her groom's house with a few kimonos. Her sister was as gentle as Grandmother. *I hope my sister will like this.* Miyuki imagined her sister with the flower crown. *She will be a pretty bride like a princess.* Miyuki's hands busily spread out a few different colored flowers, then picked the best colors and with those, she made a beautiful flower crown. She held the crown high and danced.

"Miyuki!" someone called her name. She stopped dancing and looked around.

A boy, about ten years old, appeared. He held a fish basket and a pole. His skin was dark with sunburn; his brown eyes smiled at her.

Miyuki didn't recognize him at first, but when she looked into his eyes, "Oh, Masato!" she held her breath, and almost dropped the crown. *His eyes haven't changed since he was a baby,* she thought.

Masato and Miyuki had been neighbors and played together when they were little children, but both of them grew and became busy working and seldom saw each other. When they were seven or eight, they started helping with many chores -- cooking, cleaning, washing, making vegetable gardens.

"You made a pretty crown," said Masato shyly.

"Yes, today, my sister is going to marry, so I made her a gift," she said and showed the crown to him.

"Beautiful. Well, your sister took care of me when I was a baby. I want to give her something, too…" Masato thought a while. "Oh, I will give her this fish. I caught enough today." He picked four large ones from his bamboo fish basket and, using a fishing needle, passed a string through the fishes' mouths. Soon four fish hung on the string. "Your family can eat fish for breakfast."

"Oh, such big fish! Thank you, but are you sure you have enough for yourself?"

"Yes, I caught a lot today. My lucky day." He smiled; his white teeth sparkled in the morning sun.

They were so happy for a moment together as if they had become little children again and walked home. The sun rose and they narrowed their eyes.

Masato is not a baby any longer. Miyuki remembered when they had played innocently. She smiled.

Soon they reached Miyuki's simple old flat wooden house.

"I still remember when a strong chicken ran at me so fast and pecked my foot when I was a child," said Masato.

"Yes, I remember it, too. You fell down on the ground and groaned. Your foot bled," said Miyuki.

"Yes, I still have a scar on my left foot. I didn't know that a chicken could run so fast," laughed Masato. "I was afraid of chickens for a while."

Masato handed the four fish to her. Their hands touched. Masato drew his hand away instantly. His cheeks grew hot.

Miyuki etched this into her memory, and every time she thought of it, she felt warmth in her heart like a morning sunrise.

3
Nothing to Complain About

"Such a beautiful crown," Miyuki's sister Chie, shouted with joy. Chie was a little taller than Miyuki with dark brown eyes.

"I am glad you like it," said Miyuki, and she stretched out and put the crown on Chie's head. Even though Chie wore a simple dark-colored kimono, this flower crown made her look cheerful.

"Thank you, Miyuki." Chie smiled as if she were a little girl.

"I also got four fresh fish. I will cook for you. You are a princess today, so just relax," said Miyuki. "Masato gave it to us as a wedding gift." She held out the fish for Chie to see and hurried to the kitchen.

As soon as Miyuki baked the fish, Father, Brother Sabu, Chie and Miyuki enjoyed a delicious breakfast. They usually ate only potatoes, and seldom had anything else, so this fresh tasty fish was a deluxe breakfast.

"Father, Brother, thank you for taking care of me for a long time. Miyuki, thank you for your wonderful gift. You are such a good sister to me," Chie said and bowed.

Father nodded. He looked a little lonesome, and his eyes moistened. "Serve your husband and your mother-in-law well. I know you will be a good wife."

Soon Chie was going to leave this house. *Chie was a good sister.* Miyuki remembered each memory, one after another. Chie used to comb Miyuki's hair -- she slept with Miyuki and comforted her when she had a bad dream -- she taught Miyuki how to make *origami.... I will miss her,* she thought.

Miyuki stood by the door and waved her hand. Chie smiled at her, touched the flower crown with her hand and smiled. Then she was gone.

After Chie moved out, Miyuki did the house chores all by herself—cooked, cleaned, sewed, washed, fed the chickens, worked the fields and so on. From early morning to night, she worked as hard as an ant.

Her father hadn't married again after his wife died. Sometimes he looked lonesome, but when he looked at Miyuki, he felt comforted.

"I have only potatoes for supper," said Miyuki and brought a bowl and placed it on the table. Hot boiled potatoes' smell filled the tiny room.

"Smells delicious," Father said and picked out one. "We are poor, but we can still eat."

"Yes, we have food to eat, a place to live. I can walk, I can work. I can see, I can cook, I can sing, I can eat, I can sleep, I can laugh, I can go to bathroom … our blessings are countless. We have nothing to complain…" Miyuki poured hot water into three small cups.

They couldn't afford to buy tea, so they drank hot water instead.

"You are just like Grandmother, Miyuki," Sabu said, holding the cup.

"Grandmother said we don't need many kimonos. We can only wear one at the time. It is true, isn't it?" said Miyuki. "She also said, 'There is so much wealth and so much poverty in this world, that I think we have to be satisfied with what we have right now.'"

"Yes, indeed. Miyuki is like her grandmother," nodded Father. His eyes were smiling.

Everyone laughed.

"But I wonder why there are not so many potatoes this year. We planted a lot, but I am not sure if there will be enough potatoes for the whole winter," said Sabu.

"Umm…" Father's eyes darkened.

A strong wind blew all day and became stronger at midnight.

Suddenly, someone outside shouted. "Thief!"

The villagers made noise. "Thief!" "We found the thief!"

Father, Sabu and Miyuki woke up and hurried out.

"Where?" Sabu shouted. Holding a stick, he ran as if he were a fierce dog. Father and Miyuki followed.

When Ginza tried to steal beans from his neighbor, he was caught. He was pulled violently outside. Ginza's family sat with him, tortured with terror. Then the villagers entered Ginza's house. Many strong men searched all over and found food and carried it outside.

The villagers shouted angrily when they saw it. There were so many small potatoes that they made a little mountain. Ginza couldn't have produced so many of these. He must have grown less than one tenth of these potatoes. Everyone knew how many potatoes each villager grew. Many villagers had experienced a shortage of potatoes and wondered why. Now they learned that Ginza had stolen potatoes from their garden while they were still under the soil. The angry villagers' faces became red like fire, and then they became pale and cold like ice.

Soon the potatoes were divided among the villagers.

After that day, the villagers were upset. They were much disturbed by Ginza.

"Ginza will steal our food again. We have to get revenge. Otherwise, we won't sleep well!" many villagers shouted.

"Ginza's grandfather was a thief! So his children and grandchildren tend to be thieves as well. We'd better kill them for our safety." They looked at each other and nodded.

"Ginza's family consists of thirteen people, but we have to do something!" one said quietly.

"We better make a big hole and throw them in," another said.

The villagers felt their lives were threatened and decided that someone must kill Ginza's family. The villagers were surrounded by unearthly silence.

When Miyuki heard the villagers' conversation, she grew pale and shivered like a candle's light.

"It is sad, isn't it?" she murmured.

"But Miyuki, without food, we can't survive. We must take action," Sabu said coldly.

The village was small and had little food to keep people alive, so everyone tended to get married late because early marriage meant more children. When a child was born, one old person was forced to go to God's Mountain, even though that person was not yet seventy, so the population could remain about the same.

Three days later, Miyuki heard many footsteps passing by her house and marching to the mountain. Miyuki woke up and felt chilly.

The next day, everyone knew that Ginza's family was gone from the village.

"Don't say anything about Ginza's family," one said, putting his finger to his lips. Storing food was extremely important to survive; therefore, stealing food was the worst sin in this village. They shut their mouths and most of them felt thankful for the killers.

4
A River of Joy

Miyuki placed a flower crown by the small gravestone, held her hands together and bowed. Miyuki's father had died one year earlier.

Father was very ill during his last days. His muscles ached, and he had difficulty walking. There were no doctors in this village. Miyuki always gave him her shoulder every time he needed to get up from his *futon*. She tried to make him as comfortable as she could.

"Thank you, Miyuki," Father said in a weak voice.

"You can still walk. I am glad," responded Miyuki, her voice bright as a buttercup. She was a tiny woman, but she had a lot of energy, and she seldom became sick. She worked from early morning to late evening. They were very poor, but she was always thankful for everything.

"You are just like your grandmother," Father said softly. "I am going to see her soon. My heart ached every time I remembered that I took my mother to God's Mountain. I was a bad son…"

His shoulders shook.

"Will you marry? I found a nice woman for you," Sabu's visiting aunt and asked Sabu after Father died.

"But I have to take care of Miyuki," Sabu responded.

"Miyuki is twenty-five. It is time for her to get married, too. But you must marry first," Aunty said smiling.

"Umm… I thought she was still a child," said Sabu, scratching his head.

"Time flies," said Aunty. "Her name is Yoko. She lives the next village -- a healthy, good woman."

Soon after, the aunt arranged for the marriage. One day the woman arrived with a dark brown cotton kimono. This was Sabu's wife, Yoko, a kind, hard-working woman with dark round eyes. Miyuki was happy for her brother, but she missed her father, and became lonely. Miyuki wanted to leave Sabu and Yoko alone as much as she could, so she often spent time at her father's grave.

Miyuki touched the gravestone and talked to her father. She felt he was listening.

"My brother is married. I am happy for him and his wife, but sometimes I get lonely." Miyuki said, as if Father were beside her. As she spoke, she felt relieved as she confessed her deep thought. A cherry blossom petal danced in the wind and fell on her black hair.

"Miyuki?"

She heard a voice. She looked up. "Oh! My…" Masato, who had grown to be a man, stood beside her.

"I am sorry about your father's death," he said gently, looking into her eyes.

"I heard your father died, too. How is your mother?" Miyuki looked at him and smiled.

"She is fine, and healthy as a horse. Sometimes she talks about you." His bright eyes smiled back. "I still remember your sister's wedding day. You made a crown." He looked into Miyuki's eyes. His eyes were very sincere.

"Yes, I remember. It was a long time ago, but I have never forgotten. The fish you gave me that day was so delicious," said Miyuki. Her voice danced with joy.

"I sometimes looked at you. You were always working so hard. I hesitated to call you. But your brother got married, right?" Masato looked straight into her eyes.

"Yes, his wife is a kind woman. I am glad for my brother," said Miyuki softly.

"Did you make a flower crown for her?" he asked.

"Yes indeed. She liked it very much."

"Your hands are very clever. No one can make a beautiful flower crown like you." He smiled. "Miyuki…" Suddenly his voice became serious.

"Yes?" She looked at him with her beautiful eyes.

"Miyuki, will you marry me?" he asked in musical voice. "I have been thinking about it for a long time, but you were so busy all these

17

years, taking care of your father, and I was also busy about my tasks, too. But, now your brother is married, so I think it is the right time to ask you to marry me. I will try to be a good husband."

Miyuki's chest tightened. She felt his words touch her like a gentle rain from heaven. She felt sweetness spread all over her. She had known she would marry him ever since he gave her the four fish. When her hands and his hands had touched that day, he had drawn his hands away. Miyuki knew he loved her at that moment. *It was almost fifteen years ago, but Masato still thinks of me.* Masato's love moved her profoundly. Her heart leaped with anticipation and wetted her eyes.

"Why do you cry?" asked Masato.

"My grandmother told me that tears become healing water and sometimes a river of joy," said Miyuki. "Thank you, Masato. I will try to be a good wife as well." She bowed deeply.

The warm spring sun came shining through the cherry trees and the birds sang as if they congratulated them.

The young couple stood still in a shower of sunshine as if time had stopped.

5
Eyes Tell More Than Mouth

Miyuki got up early and went to the field. The sky was blue and the sun was warm. *It was fifteen years ago,* Miyuki thought. *Time flies....* When she was ten, she received four fish from Masato. Now she was twenty-five. She smiled and started making a flower crown. When it was beautifully done, she put it on her straight black hair. She went back to her house. Yoko prepared breakfast. Miyuki remembered her sister's breakfast with four fish, fifteen years ago; now was her last breakfast in this house. She saw potatoes and dried fish on the table. Soon she would marry Masato.

"Miyuki, you're beautiful," Yoko said as she handed her a cup of hot water.

"Thank you. Please take good care of my brother," said Miyuki, smiling.

"Miyuki, you are just like Grandmother," Sabu said.

"Yes, my grandmother was a great teacher. I have never forgotten her lessons," Miyuki responded. "Brother, thank you for everything." She bowed.

"Umm... Masato is a good man. I am happy for you," Sabu said, smiling. His eyes moistened. The three of them enjoyed eating the breakfast.

And then she moved to Masato's house. She stood at the door, wearing her old cotton kimono and the flower crown that she made herself.

Masato's house was an old wooden flat house very similar to Miyuki's.

"Welcome, Miyuki," Masato's mother Fumi said and held Miyuki's hands. "You are beautiful. Just like the child I used to know. A beautiful crown, you are like a little princess. I am so glad you married my son. I have known you since you were a baby. I had been waiting for this happy day for a long time." Fumi's voice was warm and she smiled kindly.

If a rainbow could make a sound, it would sound like her voice, Miyuki thought.

"Thank you," Miyuki said softly and bowed.

Fumi and Masato bowed deeply too, and they escorted her inside the house. There was nothing much there except a strong-looking wooden table.

"Masato made this," Fumi said proudly.

"Good. He has good hands," Miyuki praised him. *A simple clean house. This will be my new home,* Miyuki thought and breathed deeply.

In the evening, Fumi invited Masato and Miyuki to the supper table.

"Looks delicious, thank you," said Miyuki. She saw dried fish, mushrooms, carrots and potatoes on the plate.

"Mother, it is a deluxe dinner. Thank you," said Masato and sat.

20

The three of them started eating. After supper, Masato played his bamboo flute. The melody flew high and low and danced in the air. Miyuki and Fumi closed their eyes and enjoyed Masato's creative music.

That night, Masato held her gently and they became one flesh. Then Miyuki slept soundly in his arms.

Fumi, Miyuki's mother-in-law, was in her late sixties. She was a kind, hard-working woman. Miyuki was happy working with her.

One day, Fumi confided to Miyuki, "We are going to go to a secret place."

Miyuki followed Fumi into a deep forest where rich water flowed into a small stream. Birds sang here and there, and the aroma of wildflowers filled the air. A cool breeze came sweeping over the river.

"I am so glad Masato and you were married. Now I can go to God's Mountain any time. But before I go, I will let you know a secret place where fish are plentiful. I learned this from my mother-in-law years ago. This is our family secret, so don't tell anyone," said Fumi, putting her finger on her lips. Her hands were rough and her nails were torn. Her skin was as rough as sand, her hair gray and thin, but she had kind, sincere eyes, just like Masato.

Soon they reached a small stream surrounded by tall grass.

"Put your hand in front of this hollow," Fumi said. "A lot of fish live here." She waded into the shallow water quietly and placed a bamboo basket in front of the hollow. Fish swam into the basket, and soon the basket was full of fish. Fumi smiled. Many wrinkles appeared on her face. Her skin was dark from sunburn, but she had dark, rounded, gentle eyes. Miyuki's grandmother used to say, "Eyes tell much more than mouth."

Indeed, she thought. *Eyes express many things. Happiness, sadness, madness, anger, kindness, gentleness, joy...* Miyuki had been observing people's eyes for years. *Does this person tell the truth or untruth?* She could know their characters through their eyes.

Grandmother also said, "The eye is the candle of the body. If your eyes are good, your whole body will be full of light."

Miyuki felt pleased when she saw her mother-in-law's gentle eyes.

"I still have very strong teeth that make me ashamed," said Fumi. "When I go to God's Mountain, I must look old and weak." She sighed. "But now I can go to God's Mountain without any worry."

"Don't go there so soon. We have a lot of fish. We can dry them and keep them for winter. You don't have to go to the mountain so soon," insisted Miyuki.

She liked Fumi. Since Miyuki's mother died, and her grandmother had gone to God's

Mountain, she felt that Fumi was like a mother to her.

All of a sudden, she remembered her grandmother in her white kimono. Her eyes moistened.

The fish in the basket jumped. Miyuki held the basket tight.

6
Kenji and the Bamboo Flute

Miyuki and Masato worked hard. They made vegetable gardens and a rice field. They picked mulberries, wild mushrooms, and fed chickens; however, even though they worked hard, they were always poor. Very often they just ate potatoes, especially during the winter. Once in a while they ate dried fish, and they felt blessed.

The soil of this village was not good, so they couldn't produce a lot of vegetables. But Miyuki didn't complain and always found some blessing. They got up with the sunrise, and worked until the sun went down. Their hard work gave them a sound sleep.

Two years earlier, Fumi had gone to God's Mountain. Masato's eyes were dark and his face paled like a dead man when he came back from God's Mountain.

That night, snow began to fall. Snowflakes kept on falling, one after another.

"Mother, it is snowing. I am happy for you," a low murmur broke from Masato's lips; he went outside.

Miyuki's chest tightened; she followed Masato. They stood still silently in the snowy night. Their hearts were broken.

But soon Miyuki was pregnant.

"It must be Mother's blessing," Masato shouted with joy. His voice danced.

The fetus grew in Miyuki's body. She touched her stomach gently and talked. Masato played the bamboo flute after supper.

On a beautiful day in June, a boy was born. Masato named him Kenji, which meant "judge cleverly."

Kenji grew healthy; his eyes were innocent, and he was obedient as a well-trained puppy. He loved flowers and often brought beautiful wildflowers home to his mother. Every time he brought flowers, Miyuki felt a warm deep love from him. She loved her son's gentle nature.

When Kenji turned five, Masato gave him a flute lesson after supper. Masato made a small bamboo flute, and son and father played together. At first, Kenji couldn't play. Even though he tried so hard, no sound came from the flute.

"Kenji, try again. Never give up!" Masato encouraged him.

Kenji tried and tried. "I can't!" His innocent eyes expressed sadness.

Miyuki felt sorry for Kenji and prayed silently.

But one night a beautiful sound jumped from Kenji's flute.

"Very good, Kenji!" Masato shouted with joy and rubbed his son's small head.

"Kenji, I am proud of you," Miyuki said and hugged him gently.

After that day, Kenji was crazy about the flute. He played every time he could. Many other children loved to play war games, but Kenji liked to play his bamboo flute. He made melodies like an angel whispering and comforting people.

Miyuki hoped this peace would last for a long time.

7
When Kenji Plays...

As Kenji's parents worked from early morning to sunset, Kenji was alone all day. He went to the mountain with his bamboo flute and a small basket. He filled it with blackberries, wild mushrooms or wild flowers and brought them home. He wanted to help his parents.

"Blackberries are juicy and tasty. Thank you, Kenji," Mother said, chewing them slowly.

Kenji was happy to please Mother, so he picked blackberries and filled the basket every day all fall. He ate and looked around. The mountain was filled with colorful leaves, red, orange, yellow... soon they would become golden and brown. He enjoyed looking at those dead leaves waltz in the wind. He sat by the blackberries patch and started to play his bamboo flute. The cool mountain air carried his beautiful melody. The sky was high and blue like the ocean. It seemed as if the many funny-shaped clouds enjoyed the music. *Beautiful*, he thought and kept on playing.

The melody flew in the air and squirrels on the tree listened peacefully. Even the birds stopped singing and turned their ears to the melodies. Silence fell on the mountain and all creatures strained their ears.

Suddenly, something moved close by. Kenji felt that someone was near. He turned around.

"Oh," he gasped, with his heart pounding in his ears and his mouth suddenly dry. He almost dropped the bamboo flute. A small brown bear sat beside Kenji and looked at him. Kenji slowly exhaled, taking another deep breath and exhaling slowly; he tried to calm himself and observed that Bear had big lonesome eyes as if he were crying. *My mother said eyes tell everything*, Kenji thought. *This is a baby bear.*

Kenji smiled at him. Then he saw that Bear's palm was bleeding. A thorn was stuck in it. He slowly drew closer. Bear sat still, so Kenji touched his palm gently, and then he removed the thick thorn from his palm. He took off his *tenugui*, a Japanese thin towel, from his neck and wiped the blood and pressed it until the bleeding stopped. Bear's eyes showed happiness.

"Are you hungry? Where is your mother?" Kenji asked.

He picked blackberries and gave them to him. Bear ate one after another, rubbing his stomach.

"You must go back to your mother," Kenji repeated. "I'll take you home. Where is your home?"

Bear looked sad and started walking slowly. Kenji followed him. The forest was dense. Trees grew close together. Birds flew from one branch to another. They crossed a little river and walked through bushes. Dead leaves on the ground made faint sounds with every step. When Kenji saw the stream, he called, "Bear, stop."

Bear stopped walking and looked back.

"Come here. I will wash your blood."

Kenji carried Bear in his arms, washed Bear's palm and cleaned the blood off. Bear was quiet in Kenji's arms. *Just like a dog,* Kenji thought. "Now you are clean."

Bear smiled at Kenji and licked his face. Kenji placed him gently on the ground. They walked about three miles. Many birds flew around them. Bear stopped. Kenji saw thick ivy hanging like curtains. On the other side was a little lake. Water flowed from a little waterfall into the lake. *Beautiful. I never knew there was such a peaceful place on this mountain,* Kenji thought.

Then Bear looked at Kenji and entered inside the ivy curtains. Surprised, Kenji followed. *No one would think there is a cave behind the ivy,* Kenji thought. At first he couldn't see anything, but soon his eyes adjusted to the darkness. The entrance was small, but inside the cave was enough space for a few bears to live comfortably. There were many dead leaves in the cave. *Just like a mattress,* Kenji chuckled.

"Is this your house? You have no Mother and Father?"

Bear looked at Kenji with his innocent eyes.

"Okay, I am your brother now. You are not lonely anymore." Kenji stroked Bear's head. Bear licked Kenji's hands.

After that day, Kenji and Bear became friends. Every time he played his bamboo flute by the blackberry patch, Bear appeared and played and they ate the berries together.

"This is our secret," Kenji said. "If the villagers knew it, they would kill you, so I haven't told anyone." Kenji put his finger to his lips. "Winter is coming soon. You must eat a lot before your winter sleeping. We will see you next spring. When I play the flute, you come out, okay? Sleep well."

Kenji patted Bear's neck. Bear stood up and hugged him. Kenji felt the warmth of Bear's fur.

That night, snowflakes danced all over and made everywhere as white as if the world was covered with a white carpet. Kenji loved the silence of a snow day. He felt wrapped in quietness.

The snow continued falling. Snow fairies danced a waltz and a soft white veil fell over the mountains, the trees, the cave and Kenji's house.

Bear must be sleeping in the cave by now. Kenji missed Bear, and he couldn't wait for spring.

"Good night, Bear… Sleep well…"

Soon Bear grew and he became big enough to carry Kenji on his back. Sometimes Kenji rode on Bear's back as if he were riding a horse. They wrestled too, and they napped together in the cave. Their friendship grew as if they were a master and a faithful dog.

One beautiful fall day, they met by the blackberry patch as usual. They ate, and then Kenji started playing flute. Bear danced and wild animals came closer. Dead leaves flew in the wind. The sun gave a thin light and made a beautiful afternoon.

"Child, don't move!" Kenji heard a loud voice. He stopped playing and looked back. A samurai held a bow and arrow aimed toward Bear.

"No!" Kenji cried and ran toward the samurai, trying to protect Bear. "Bear, run!" he ordered. Bear glanced at Kenji, and then ran toward the bushes. An arrow flew and hit Bear, but he ran off.

"Shame on you!" the samurai shouted. "I almost caught a bear!" He glared at Kenji; his face red as fire, and spat.

Kenji waited until the samurai was gone. Then he hurried to the cave. Bear was there and lay on the dead leaves. Blood came from a stomach wound. "Bear!" Kenji cried. Bear's breath was rough. Kenji went outside and dipped his *tenugui* in the lake. He ran back to the cave and wet Bear's mouth. "Don't die!"

Kenji held Bear's hand and lay beside him. Bear looked at Kenji tenderly as Kenji held his paw. "Don't die! Bear..." as if he were praying. "We can be good friends for many more years." Bear couldn't breathe; he looked at Kenji one last time and closed his eyes. He was gone.

"Bear!" Kenji hugged Bear. He felt as if someone had stuck a needle into his heart. "Wake up, Bear! God, please let him live." He shook Bear and looked at for him for a long time. "Bear, you were a little baby when we met the first time. You're a good dancer. Why don't you wake up?" Kenji talked and talked as if he were waiting for Bear to wake up.

Finally Kenji admitted Bear was dead.

"Bear, thank you for being a good friend. Now you can see your father and mother in the bear heaven. Please watch over me from above," Kenji murmured.

When he left the cave, it was dark and the stars and moon shone in the ultramarine sky. His eyes were red but dry. He drank water. After he had cried so much, his body was dehydrated. The cold water refreshed him. He started home. When he reached the blackberry patch, he heard Father's voice.

"Kenji, where have you been? You didn't come home for supper. We were worried about you."

Suddenly, Kenji hugged Father's chest; his cheeks were full of tears again and wet Father's kimono.

"What's the matter with you?" Father asked gently and stroked Kenji's back.

"I am sorry Father, I didn't tell you this before but..." Kenji's story began.

Amazed, Father listened quietly. After Kenji told about Bear, Father said, "You must bury Bear."

"Yes, I have to bring a tool to dig the hole," Kenji said.

"I will help you. Carrying a big bear is a hard job. You will need help. Let's get tools," Father said.

Kenji nodded. "But Father, don't tell anyone about Bear. I just want to let him sleep peacefully."

After they got the tools, Kenji led Father to the cave where Bear slept. Father and Kenji dug a big hole near the cave and carried out Bear and buried him. Stardust and the moon gently sent their light.

Kenji played his bamboo flute as a farewell to Bear. The beautiful sad melody flew in the cool, quiet autumn air.

8
Not Yet, Miyuki

Kenji and Masato were in the mountains gathering wood branches for fuel for the winter. The top of the mountains was enveloped in mist and the visibility was zero. Now Kenji was old enough to help his father. He missed Bear, but he was very busy working with his father, so he seldom visited the cave. But he always remembered Bear in his deepest heart.

"It's dangerous to work in such darkness. We better go back," Masato said. They carried wooden branches on their backs.

It had rained for a week, so the ground was wet and soft and made their steps difficult. They walked a while. Even though it was dark, they knew how to get home, as they had come to this mountain many times.

"Woof, woof..." They heard deep growls.

"Wolf!" Masato became tense, instantly; he stood on guard. They threw away their wood branches from their shoulders and held their canes and stood strong, shoulder to shoulder. They were surrounded by several wolves.

Suddenly, the lead wolf ran toward Kenji. Masato pushed Kenji away to protect him. Then the wolf's sharp nails struck Masato's face. Masato tried to avoid the wolf's attack and bent backward. The next moment, the wolf bit his throat. Masato tried to beat off the wolf, but the wolf knocked him down to the ground.

Kenji gasped. Masato and the wolf were fighting on the ground. Kenji tried to calm the wolf, and ordered him in a dignified voice:

"Go away! Don't hurt my father! You must leave."

The wolf glared at Kenji. He repeated, "You must leave right now!" Just as if he were talking to Bear. When Bear and Kenji had become friends, he learned many things about how to treat animals. He learned how to get Bear to follow his instructions. Kenji was Bear's master, and Bear always followed Kenji's order. Kenji's voice had power.

They looked at each other. The other wolves stood quietly. Then Kenji remembered he had a flute in a small sack on his hip. He grabbed the flute and started to play as if he were playing to Bear. The melody ran in the misty air and seemed to calm the wolves.

"Woof!" the wolf barked once, and then they left, one by one, and all disappeared.

Kenji ran toward his father and touched his neck. Blood wet his hands.

"Take care of your mother, Kenji," Father whispered, his voice was as thin as a string.

"Father!" Kenji's cry echoed in the quiet mountains.

After Masato died, Miyuki and Kenji's bond became much stronger. Miyuki taught all her wisdom and experience that came from her grandmother to Kenji. Kenji was a good listener, just like Miyuki when she was a child, and he loved and respected his mother deeply. Miyuki was his mother, but sometimes she became his father as well.

I hope Kenji will have a good wife; he is thirty-five, Miyuki thought. But Kenji didn't mention anything about it.

Miyuki's grandmother had been gone for a long time. Now, Miyuki was an old woman. *This will be my last spring; time has flown.* When winter came, she would be seventy. Miyuki opened the shoji sliding door and looked outside at the green mountains. Birds sang and flowers were beginning to open. Fresh air danced into the room and filled it with a sweet aroma. Miyuki closed her eyes and enjoyed the fragrance of spring.

"Good morning, Mother." Kenji came into the room. He was slim and tall. He was always quiet and cool as water, but his dark brown eyes under thick eyebrows were warm.

"I will be seventy soon, and it is time to go to God's Mountain," Miyuki said in a calm tone.

"No!" cried Kenji. "You must not go there, not yet."

"My mother-in-law and my grandmother went there. Now it is time for me." Miyuki knew Kenji's heart. Although he was thirty-five, he had the heart of a child. He always cared for Miyuki as if he were her husband or Father.

"When my grandmother went to God's Mountain, it began to snow. She had soft, silver hair and wore a simple white kimono. She was calm as a sleeping baby. When I go to the mountain, I hope it will snow. My mother told me a god lived in this mountain.

"My grandmother said she would feel lucky if the snow would start falling when she arrived there. She wanted to lie on the cold mountain snow, and die," said Miyuki, remembering her last farewell.

"Dying on a snow day is the best way to go, but I don't agree with Lord Higashi's rule, even though he is the leader of our village," cried Kenji. Then he stood up and left the room as if he were an angry tiger.

Miyuki looked at his back. *He is just like his father,* she thought. She turned her eyes to the outside. *I was married in spring, on a beautiful day like today.* She closed her eyes, and she revered her husband.

I will be seventy. I must go to God's Mountain soon. It was as if she were talking to her husband. The corners of her eyes had a few wrinkles, but she still had the innocent gaze of a child.

Masato ... I will see you soon. It has been a long time since you left. But I am still lucky to have my son. He is so sweet and my comfort. She kept her eyes closed and meditated. Soon she heard Masato's voice.

Not yet, Miyuki. You have more duties to do. You must live to do my part, too.

But I am almost seventy. As soon as Kenji marries a nice woman, I am ready to go and be with you.

Not yet, Miyuki. Not yet... Masato's smile was like a golden sun.

She slowly opened her eyes. She heard birds' singing.

"Am I dreaming?" Miyuki smiled.

Cherry petals danced in the wind and fell on the ground; soon those petals made a pink carpet.

9
Thanks, Bear!

On the eve of Miyuki's farewell, she invited four people who had taken relatives to God's Mountain before. For years, Miyuki had prepared and saved sake, rice and dried fish for her farewell ceremony. Everyone sat quietly.

The oldest person sat in the best seat and taught Kenji the rules associated with going to God's Mountain.

"Neither of you is allowed to talk," the first man said after he drank from the sake cup. He seemed to be in the early sixties. His voice vibrated into the cold air as if he were afraid of something. He must have been thinking that he himself would be going to God's Mountain sooner or later. He closed his eyes and thought of when he took his mother to the mountain. His eyes darkened.

Kenji's face was pale; his shoulders trembled.

The next man said, "When you leave the house, make sure nobody sees you." Then he received the sake cup from the first man and drank, as if he were trying to forget the day he took his mother to the mountain. As he drank the sake so quickly, he choked.

The third man said in a low voice, "When you return, do not look back," and drank the sake slowly. He seemed to be in his mid-forties. He had taken his mother to God's Mountain last year. He held the sake cup with his head hung low.

The fourth man taught Kenji how to get to the mountain. His eyes turned dark as if he were telling him a bad thing.

Everyone became quiet. For a minute, time seemed to stop. They had nothing more to say. Soon they finished eating and drinking; then everyone bowed. Miyuki smiled and bowed back.

After the four guests left, Miyuki asked Kenji to play his bamboo flute. He nodded and started to play. The flute made a melody that was beautiful, full of sorrow, sounding almost like a prayer. Miyuki closed her eyes and listened. *This is the last day I can listen to his flute.* Miyuki remembered how Kenji grew. After she became a widow, she worked as a farmer and taught all her wisdom to Kenji. They were poor, but their home had peace.

The beautiful melody flew in the air.

At midnight, Kenji carried Miyuki on his back, walking under the moonlight. Neither spoke. They crossed a valley and a lake. At last they reached God's Mountain. At the mountain, an unearthly silence overwhelmed Kenji. He breathed deeply and climbed the steep slope. He felt as if his heart were bleeding.

When they passed a big stone, they saw a body and black birds. They saw many bones. Suddenly, a dead body moved. Kenji gasped.

Then he saw a black bird came out from the dead men's kimono. *Oh, the blackbird was eating the dead body,* he thought. Then another black bird came out from the dead man's kimono sleeve.

Miyuki was shocked when she saw these black birds. *Is this God's Mountain? I don't see any gods. Will these blackbirds eat my body after I die? My grandmother told me God's Mountain was a holy place, and I believed her. But it is a human boneyard. Some of these bones might be my grandmother's. Grandmother, you must have been lonely dying in such a place. But I am going to be with you soon.*

It is getting dark. After Kenji leaves me here, will he able to go home?

Miyuki worried about her son.

When Kenji saw these dead bodies, bones and black birds, he couldn't stand to leave his mother in such a place.

I can't! I can't! I can't. Father, please give me your wisdom. Kenji's heart was heavy as if it were a stone. *Should I take her somewhere and hide? But where? God help me. Please give me your mercy!* he moaned to God. All of a sudden, he saw Bear, who was smiling at Kenji in the air. "Oh, thanks, Bear!" Kenji shouted with joy.

Kenji stopped climbing. "Mother! I can't do it. Since my father died, you took care of me by yourself. You are my mother and sometimes you are my father. When I was sick, you didn't sleep and instead took care of me. Why should I throw you away and leave you alone in such a scary place?"

Miyuki hugged Kenji gently, "You must leave me here. Do not go against Lord Higashi's order. My grandmother and Mother-in-Law came here, too. Leave me on the big stone. It will snow soon. I will lie down on the snow and sleep. Soon I will die. Go home now!"

"Mother, I can't leave you here. I know a nice cave near the village. When I was a child, I found it. It was a secret place. Nobody knew except my father and Bear. I just now remembered it. It must be God's idea. Why didn't I think of this before? I will hide you there. I will bring food, a mat, and a warm kimono."

"Kenji..." Miyuki was so touched; she couldn't utter a word.

Kenji carried Miyuki on his shoulders, going back the way they came. They had to arrive at the secret place before sunrise. Kenji walked as fast as he could, sweat dripping from his face. He was almost running.

God, please protect Kenij, Miyuki prayed silently. Then she heard her husband's voice. "Not yet, Miyuki. Not yet…"

10
The Cave

The cave was a perfect place to hide. The very small entrance was covered with ivy. Only one person could enter at a time, but inside the cave was much larger.

There was a stream near the cave, so she could drink water and wash her hands. The little lake was as beautiful and calm as if it were a smooth mirror. She saw a deep forest ahead, and a mountain range covered by snow. The sun that hit her skin was cool, but not too cold, and the cool morning air refreshed Miyuki's soul.

Beside the cave, there was a small gravestone for Bear. Kenji spoke about Bear passionately, and Miyuki listened quietly and smiled.

Kenji returned to the village and brought food, a wooden bowl, chopsticks, candles, a flint, a straw mat and a warm cotton kimono. He also brought a small hibachi and charcoal, so she could get warm. Kenji placed the straw mat on a pile of dead leaves.

"This is wonderful, Kenji. Thank you." Miyuki bowed, expressing appreciation.

"I will bring food every day. It is cold now, but be patient. Very soon spring will come. If I had left you on the mountain, I would have felt guilty. Mother, you are still healthy. You will be able to live in the cave. If Lord Higashi were to find out my deed, he would kill me in your place." Kenji smiled.

After Kenji left, Miyuki opened the ivy curtain and looked outside. The snow had stopped and stars shone in the aquamarine sky. "I was supposed to die, but I didn't. It must be God's will. God, please protect Kenji." Miyuki bowed and prayed.

She was tired, so she lay on the straw mat. It was soft and comfortable. Soon Miyuki closed her eyes, and slept soundly.

Not yet, Miyuki, Not yet. You have many more things to do, Miyuki heard her husband's voice.

"But what do I have to do? I am an old woman now," Miyuki murmured.

Every day, Kenji ate half his food and brought the other half to Miyuki. When spring came, Miyuki went out at night and caught a lot of fish from the river, dried them and kept them in the cave.

When Kenji visited, she gave him dried fish. "I am old, so I don't need much. You are young; you need more food."

Every time Kenji found beautiful wildflowers, he brought them to Miyuki. Her cave was full of them. Miyuki made a flower crown and placed it on Bear's small gravestone. "Bear, thank you," Miyuki said and washed the gravestone with water.

Miyuki seemed to be adjusting well to living in this cave. "I am like a bear, but it's not too bad to live like this. God, thank you for everything."

11
Samurai Powers

Nobody knew that Miyuki was hiding in the cave. She didn't go out much, but at night, she enjoyed looking at stars and moonlight. She didn't have many things to do in this cave. As she used to work so hard, she had not had enough time to enjoy the beauty of nature. Now she had much time to enjoy it. She didn't know how to write haiku or waka, Japanese poems, but she spoke from her heart every time she was touched by nature. Sometimes deer came to drink water in the stream. Miyuki watched them near the cave.

Soon a deer came closer to Miyuki. She stroked the deer's neck gently. *If Bear still lived, would he become my friend, too?* Miyuki smiled as if she were a little girl again.

During the fifteenth and sixteenth centuries, many samurai warriors increased their powers and fought to become the lord of Japan. After Ashikaga Shogun collapsed, Takeda, Uesugi, Imari, Oda, Akechi, Hashiba, Tokugawa, and many other samurai fought to become the lord of Japan. Takeda Shingen was one of the strongest samurai who lived in the mountains. Even though his enemies attacked him, he was always as cool as a big mountain and ordered, "Do not move!"

During the winter, his mountain was surrounded by snow, so his enemies couldn't attack him. It was impossible to beat him until Oda imported guns. After Takeda Shingen died, his son Katsuya fought against Oda. Katsuya's army used bows and arrows, and Oda's army used guns. Oda was the first samurai leader in Japan to use guns.

Before the samurai fought with guns, war was emotional and elegant. Once, the samurai who lived in the mountains ran out of salt. "Without salt, they can't fight." His enemy, who lived near the sea, sent salt to his enemy before the war.

When a samurai fought against another samurai, they introduced themselves before the battle, and the winner chopped off his enemy's head and brought it home. His wife cleaned and combed it carefully. Maybe tomorrow, her own husband's head would be chopped off, and his enemy's wife would be careful of it. But, since Lord Oda started using guns, war strategy had changed. There was no more elegance, just force.

Lord Oda came from a small province. When he was still a young man, powerful Lord Imari's army tied to attack Oda. Lord Oda had an army of 4,000 and had to stand against the 40,000 of Imari's army. It seemed impossible for Oda to beat Imari. But a young Oda had studied his enemy's situation, condition and state of affairs. He found out the Imari army was eating lunch. At that moment, the 4,000 of Oda's army attacked the 40, 000 of Imari's. The Imari army was not ready to fight. They thought they had won the war, so they had eaten and drunk sake; it was a very hot humid day, so many samurai were naked and some of them asleep. Lord Oda ordered his samurai to kill only Lord Imari. Two found him and cut off his head.

Everyone thought Lord Oda was a genius of war. He married his enemy's daughter, and they became devoted couple. She was a very intelligent and beautiful woman; however, she didn't have any children. Oda almost became the Lord of Japan, but because of his cruelty, he was killed by his vassal, Akechi Mitsuhide.

Lord Hashiba, a tiny monkey like person, came from a poor peasant background. But with his wisdom, he became the Lord of Japan after Lord Oda died.

Lord Hashiba was Lord Oda's subordinate. When Lord Oda came out of a room, Hashiba gave him warm slippers. Lord Oda thought Hashiba had sat on his slippers and got angry. Hashiba replied calmly, "Oh, no, my lord. Why could I sit on your slippers? I put them to my chest and hugged them."

One day, Lord Oda visited Hashiba's house. Sweat dropped from Lord Oda's forehead because his horse had run for hours. Hashiba gave him a cup of cold tea first, then a cup of warm tea; and finally he served him a cup of hot tea. Lord Oda asked why? Hashiba said, "At first, you were very thirsty, so I gave you a cup of cold tea. Then you felt better, so I gave you a cup of warm tea. Then you were ready to taste steamy tea, so I served a hot steamy tea last." Lord Oda praised Hashiba's thoughtfulness.

Lord Tokugawa was a powerful and patient man. He met Lord Oda when he was a little boy; Lord Oda impressed Tokugawa's strong will, and they became friends. Lord Oda, Lord Hashiba and Lord Tokugawa wrote poems. Each poem expressed their characters.

"If you don't sing, I will kill you, little cuckoo," wrote Lord Oda.

"If you don't sing, I will find a way to make you sing, little cuckoo," wrote Lord Hashiba.

"If you don't sing, I will wait until you sing, little cuckoo," wrote Lord Tokugawa.

Finally the patient man, Lord Tokugawa, became first Tokugawa Shogun. He wrote instructions for his sons, and they followed his teaching. The Tokugawa Shogun, the Lord of Japan, prospered for 260 years.

Lord Toraga was another province's samurai leader at that time. He gained his power with his wisdom. He was smart and powerful and a deep thinker. His army was brave, and they fought for their master sincerely. His soldiers didn't mind dying for their master. When Lord Toraga was only seven, he became a hostage, so his subordinates cared for his castle. They worked hard and saved gold for Lord Toraga. Many years later, Lord Toraga came back to his castle and learned that his subordinates had kept the castle in good condition and saved gold for him. Lord Toraga appreciated them.

He learned patience through his long hostage experience, and he was very careful about spending money.

His kimono was simple. He ate rice, miso soup and no more than one additional dish. His hobby was hunting. While he hunted, he could observe the villagers' conditions, also he could eat deer or birds after he hunted them. His snack was only rice crackers. He was a very practical man with deep thoughts. He was like a bulldog; many people couldn't figure out what was he thinking.

His first wife came from a very powerful samurai family. She was a princess, and she bore a son who was much smarter and braver than his father; however, she didn't get along with her husband. At that time, most of the high ranking samurais had mistresses in order to have many sons for war. Lord Toraga had many mistresses, but he always chose women from the lower classes. He must have thought that lower class women wouldn't spend much money.

Once, Lord Toraga visited Lord Oda's castle. When Lord Oda's wife saw Lord Toraga's simple kimono, she pitied him. Moreover, his subordinates' kimonos material had been so thin, held against the light, she could see patches sewn on here and there. However, Lord Toraga brought a lot of gold as a souvenir to Lord Oda. Lord Oda's wife made Lord Toraga and his subordinates new kimonos and gave them as gifts.

Lord Toraga thanked her for them, but he was not at all ashamed of his simple looks. He didn't like to spend for any luxury; he preferred to save money for war or emergency. He saved a lot of gold in his castle.

He always tried to win without fighting if he could.

Lord Higashi was an intelligent leader as well, but he was more a poet than a samurai. He was thin and tall. He wrote haiku and waka. He was also an artist.

He didn't remember his mother. His mother had married into a stronger samurai leader's order. As she was a very gentle woman, she was loved by her husband. When he became sick, she recommended he drink milk. At that time, nobody drank it. First, she drank, then gave the cup to him. He smiled and received it. They were a devoted couple;

however, soon after she bore a son, she was torn from her loving husband by force. The husband was ordered to marry another woman. They got married, but he never visited her room. Instead, he just remembered his first wife and escaped into reading and writing waka and haiku.

Lord Higashi grew up to be like his father.

His army was not strong. They just protected their poor village. He lived on small taxes from his villagers. He was a sensitive man. His heart ached when older people had to go to God's Mountain, but he didn't know how to prevent it. Going to God's Mountain to die had a long history. As his village was extremely poor, he had no courage to change this sad custom:

"I am weak."

Sometimes he hated himself and sighed.

12
The Puzzle

The remains of last night's gray sky was dyed many colors by a golden morning sun. There was a short summer, maybe only two weeks a year, in this area. The villagers enjoyed the vivid green earth under the sun. But this beautiful summer day changed into a hell. Who could predict in such a thing?

Villagers heard horses galloping, and the sound became louder and louder. They seemed to be coming toward them.

"War?"

The villagers' faces became pale.

"Oh, Toraga! Lord Toraga's army is coming!" someone shouted when he saw flags. Many soldiers held these flags, on which was written "Toraga."

"No!" someone cried out.

"Toraga is the powerful samurai leader. Is he going to kill us?" another shouted.

Soon Toraga's army reached Lord Higashi's castle, which was like an old temple.

Lord Higashi's soldiers shivered when they saw Toraga's army. *Lord Toraga's soldiers are strong and brave. Nobody can defeat them.*

Lord Toraga got off his horse and said, "I would like to meet Lord Higashi." His voice was strong and powerful like a drum.

Lord Higashi came to an entrance of his castle and stood against Lord Toraga. Many brave samurais stood behind Lord Toraga; horses neighed.

"Well…" Lord Toraga said. "I don't like war. If possible, I want to avoid it."

Lord Higashi nodded silently and waited.

"So, I brought you a puzzle. If you solve this puzzle, your villagers are safe. But if you can't solve it, your village has to belong to me. I have seventy times as many soldiers, and they are much stronger than yours."

He showed a wooden ball to Lord Higashi. It was ten inches in diameter, and there were two small holes drilled into the ball. A winding tunnel inside connected those holes.

If you can put a string through this tunnel," Toraga said, "I will not disturb you anymore. I give you seven days. If you can't solve it, your whole village will belong to me and must pay me taxes." Lord Toraga sneered. His deep voice resounded. Lord Higashi's soldiers lost their courage.

Lord Toraga laughed loudly. And then, his army suddenly left. It was as if a strong wind had blown through the village.

As soon as Lord Toraga's soldiers left, the villagers heard this news, they were horrified. They tried to solve the puzzle. They thought and thought, but nobody could find the answer.

"Our Lord Higashi can't beat Lord Toraga in battle." the villagers moaned. "We are so poor, how can we pay expensive taxes? We will have to die."

13
Miyuki's Wisdom

Miyuki was watching ants. *Ants are small, but hard workers,* she remembered Grandmother's words. *Do they sleep under the ground during winter just like bears?*

She made a flower crown and replaced it on *Bear's* small tombstone. *If you hadn't met Kenji, I would not be living here. How thoughtful God is.*

Yesterday's sun was strong, so the fish that Miyuki placed outside was dried well. She put one dried fish beside the flower crown. She closed her eyes and remembered when she made a flower crown for her sister's wedding. Every time she meditated, her husband, Masato, came into her dream. *Then you gave me four fish,* she thought. *When can I go to your place?*

Not yet, Miyuki, she heard his whispering voice.

But why? she asked.

You will know soon. I am proud of you. Masato smiled.

The sun was warm and the sky was blue like a beautiful lake. Miyuki looked at the stream. She saw her own image on the water's surface, and Masato's. *Is it a dream?* If it were a dream, she didn't want to wake up. She gently looked back. Kenji stood behind her. "Oh, Kenji," Miyuki said gently. Kenji handed food to her as usual.

As she observed Kenji, she felt something different. "What is the matter with you?" she asked.

"Mother, Lord Toraga came to our village and gave us a puzzle…"

"Puzzle?"

Kenji told her about it. Miyuki listened carefully. After she heard it, she thought a while and smiled. "My grandmother taught me this when I was a child… . It is easy."

"Mother! Do you know the answer?" Kenji's eyes grew wide.

Miyuki smiled and told him what to do.

"Mother! You are a smart woman. I must tell this good news to Lord Higashi!"

14
An Ant

The seventh day arrived. The sun rose from the east. It was a fine day.

Soon after the sunrise, Lord Toraga, fully clad in armor, arrived with his soldiers. *Without war, I don't have to spend money. I will have another tax from this province, so I can save more*, he chuckled to himself.

"Can anyone solve this puzzle?" Lord Toraga laughed, as he held the wooden ball high. The villagers' eyes closed in despair. They looked at the wooden ball silently and hopelessly. Lord Toraga repeated, "Nobody?"

"Yes, sir," Kenji said clearly, and made his way to the front of the gathering.

"Oh!" a stir ran through the villagers. They looked at Kenji as if he were a god.

Soon he stood in front of Lord Toraga and received the wooden ball into his hands. Everyone held their breath and looked at Kenji and the wooden ball.

Kenji took a deep breath. He opened a small box. He gently placed a small ant with a delicate silken string tied to his body into one of the holes, and soon the ant came out the other side of the ball. Kenji removed the string from the ant and held the ball up high for all to see. The string dangled from both holes.

Lord Toraga's face turned red, then blue. "What a smart man! Very well!"

Soon he left the village like an angry elephant. His soldiers followed him.

He never disturbed Lord Higashi's province again.

Lord Higashi and the villagers shouted with joy, "Banzai! Banzai!" They clapped their hands.

"Since you saved our village, I will grant you any wish," Lord Higashi said warmly.

"Anything I want?" Kenji's eyes grew wide.

"Yes, I promise," replied Lord Higashi.

Kenji sat down on the ground and said, "This is not my wisdom, but my mother's. Last year, I took her to God's Mountain, and I almost left her there, but I couldn't. So I brought her back and hid her in a cave. If she had died last year, nobody here could have solved this puzzle. Her experience and wisdom saved our village. Please respect our older people. I just couldn't leave my mother to die on the mountain. She is my mother, who gave me life. If you still insist she must go to the mountain, please kill me instead." Kenji touched his hands on the ground and bowed in respect.

Lord Higashi looked at Kenji, "Your true love for your mother saved us." Lord Higashi was touched profoundly by Kenji's attitude. "You can bring your mother home." Then he looked at the villagers and ordered, "From now on, nobody has to take his older parents to the mountain. We must protect the old. We must respect their experience and wisdom. We must honor our parents' love. We must try hard to produce more food, and if someone knows the secret, we must share our wisdom. We must try hard to produce food."

The villagers were surprised. They shouted with joy.

"Kenji, thank you. I learned an excellent lesson from you." Lord Higashi bowed deeply.

The villagers clapped their hands, joyfully. They were moved by Lord Higashi's order.

"Mother!" Kenji's eyes were blurred by tears.

Suddenly, he ran to the cave.

Epilogue

Miyuki came back from the cave. Every one welcomed her. Seventy-one years old, Miyuki, still healthy with a sharp mind, was called, "the clever woman." Many people came to ask her advice whenever they needed it, even Lord Higashi. As he had grown up without his mother, he grew to look on Miyuki as his own mother. Every time he visited her, he brought some souvenir, and he was amazed by her wisdom.

Everyone applied their wisdom and experience to produce more food. The villagers worked hard as a team. Gradually, the village produced more food.

Kenji married a clever hard-working woman, just like his mother Miyuki; she saw her grandchildren and a great-grandchild. Miyuki heard joyful children's voices each time she came out of her house. Miyuki was pleased

Morning dew covered the field. Every time sun hit the dew, it shone as if it were crystal.

"Beautiful," Miyuki studied it and sighed.

She got up early and left her house. She was going to visit the cave where she used to live. She walked slowly, enjoying the birds' singing. Wildflower fragrance tickled Miyuki's nose. Her hair had turned to silver, her body had grown smaller, but she could still walk. *Thank you, God,* she murmured.

Squirrels and wild rabbits ran near her. Sometimes they stopped and looked at her. She stopped walking and looked at the sky. White clouds floated in the blue sky. Each shape was different. When she was a child, she had enjoyed looking at them. The clouds were like an apple, a flower or a potato. But today, she saw a cloud just like her husband Masato's face. She smiled.

She started walking again, slowly as if she were a turtle, rested a while, and wiped her sweating face. Finally, she reached the cave. A deer drank water. She walked closer, and waved her hand. The deer recognized her. She touched the ivy curtains and went into the cave.

She waited for a while in order to adjust her eyes to the darkness. The cave had not changed since she was gone. She touched dead leaves on the floor. *This cave saved my life,* she thought. *How thoughtful God is!*

She placed a white wildflower by Bear's tombstone, and then she stood by the stream. Her reflection was on the water's surface. Time had stopped. A young Masato and Miyuki, with her flower crown, were reflected on the water, as if they had just been married. She held her breath. *Am I dreaming?* She wondered.

Masato, I am ready. When will you pick me up?

You did very well, Miyuki. I am proud of you. Now is the time to be together. Come with me. She heard Masato's voice. Then she felt as if she were held by Masato's strong arms. *Come with me.* Masato repeated. She felt as if she were surrounded by a golden cloth woven from Masato's love and gentleness. She was deeply moved. The next moment, she felt she was flying in the air with Masato.

Miyuki closed her eyes and smiled.

Thank you for everything.

About the Author

Midori Bamba is a member of Hampton Roads Writers, James River Writers, Virginia Beach Writers, Great Neck Book Club, and SCBWI (Society of Children both Writers and Illustrators).

Ms. Bamba has published more than thirty articles in magazines, books and the Virginian-Pilot newspaper. She has self published *The Three Sailors* in 2011 and *The Three Survivors* by Snowflake in 2010.

Midori Bamba likes to laugh, to cry and to learn when she reads. She likes John Grisham, John Steinbeck. Philippa Gregory, Tolstoy, Billy Graham and many other authors. Ms. Bamba also likes self-help books. Her favorite books are *Daddy Long Legs*, *Secret Garden,* and *Gone with the Wind.*

Ms. Bamba grew up in Sapporo, Japan. She was surrounded by snow from November to March. She feels a snowflake is the most beautiful of God's creations.

Ms. Bamba loves reading and writing and making veggie gardens.

Midori Bamba currently lives in Virginia Beach, Virginia with her six-year-old dog, Sylvie.